Translated from the Portuguese
A casa que voou

First published in the United Kingdom
in 2016 by Thames & Hudson Ltd,
181A High Holborn, London WC1V 7QX

Text © 2015 Davide Cali
Illustrations © 2015 Catarina Sobral
Original edition © 2015 Bruaá Editora
This edition © 2016 Thames & Hudson Ltd,
London

British Library Cataloguing-
in-Publication Data
A catalogue record for this book
is available from the British Library

ISBN 978-0-500-65094-3

Printed in Portugal

To find out about all our publications,
please visit **www.thamesandhudson.com**.
There you can subscribe to our e-newsletter,
browse or download our current catalogue,
and buy any titles that are in print.

Davide Cali
Catarina Sobral

The House That Flew Away

 Thames & Hudson

Once upon a time, there was a house that flew away.
It simply rose up from the ground one day and soared into the air.

This was very strange indeed.
The house had never done
anything like it before.

Its owner was amazed. He'd never heard of this happening to anyone else. He'd always believed that houses stayed in one place. Well, unless they had wheels and were called caravans, that is.

The owner went to the local police station for help.
'Excuse me, officer,' he said. 'Can you help me?
My house has flown away.'

'What's that?' said the policeman.
'Do you mean somebody's stolen it?'

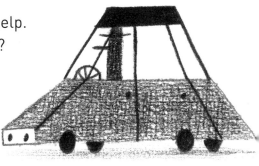

The owner shook his head.
'No, the house just flew away, all by itself.'

'Well, we can't help with that,' said the policeman.
'Perhaps you should try the Office of Natural Disasters.'

So the owner went to the Office of Natural Disasters.
'Can you help me?' he said. 'My house has flown away.'

'That's very odd,' said the kind lady at the counter.
'Our weather forecast said nothing about a tornado today.'

'There was no tornado,' explained the owner.
'The house just flew away, all by itself.'

'Well, if it wasn't a tornado, we can't help,' said the lady.
'Perhaps you should try the Lost Property Office.'

So the owner went to the Lost Property Office.
'Can you help me?' he said. 'My house has flown away.'

'Do you mean you've lost it?' said the man at the desk.

'No, it's not lost,' explained the owner. 'The house just flew away,
all by itself. Look out of the window and you'll see it flying by!'

'Well, if you know where it is, it isn't really lost,'
said the man at the desk. 'Things have to be lost
to be found, so we can't help you. Perhaps you
should try the Office of Air Traffic Control.'

So the owner went to the Office of
Air Traffic Control. 'Can you help me?'
he said. 'My house has flown away.'

'As long as it has a valid flying licence, that's
not a problem at all, sir,' said the clerk.

'But it doesn't have a flying licence,' explained the owner.
'It's never flown anywhere before; it's always been fixed
to the ground. But today it just flew away, all by itself.
Now I don't know what to do.'

'Well, we can't help you,' said the clerk. 'In fact, we should make you pay a fine for letting your house fly without a licence. But since you've got enough trouble to deal with today, we'll let it go this time.'

'But who will help me now?' asked the owner. 'I've been everywhere and asked everyone.'

'Perhaps the house had a reason for flying away,' suggested the clerk. 'Perhaps you should go and think about it.'

OFFICE OF AIR TRAFFIC CONTROL

The owner was rather upset now.
His house was sailing through the
sky and he couldn't do a thing about it.

Up above, the house flew further and further away.

Soon it was leaving the town behind.

The owner jumped in
his car and began to
follow it. He followed
it all day.

He followed it all night.
Then he followed it all the next day too.

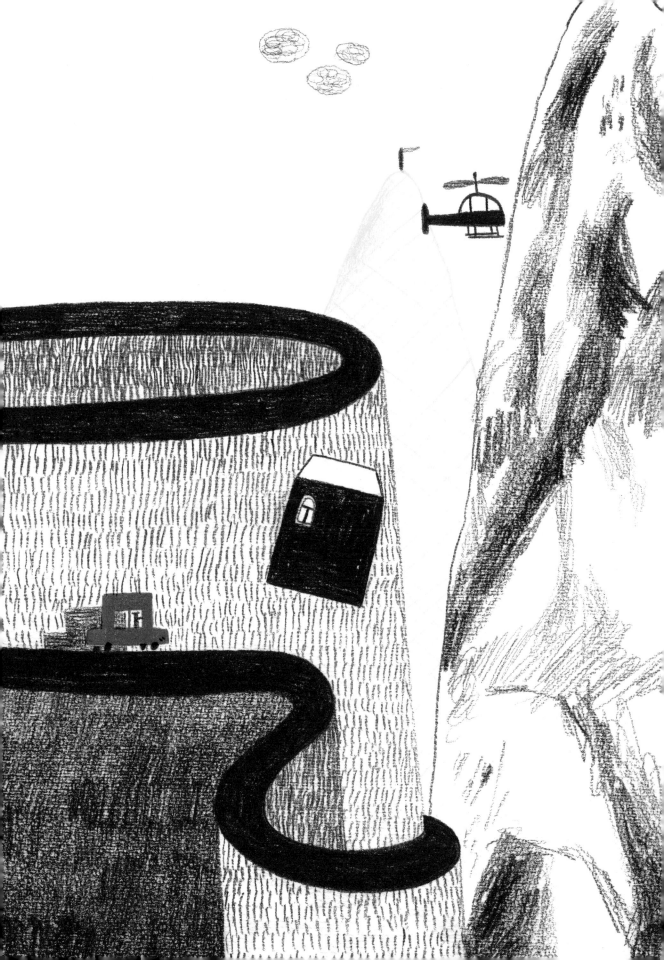

Suddenly, the owner recognized the road he was driving on. It was the road that led to his aunt and uncle's house. When he was a little boy, he had gone there every summer and had a wonderful time. But his aunt and uncle had moved away and the old house had been knocked down. The owner hadn't been back there for years and years.

The owner watched as the flying house
floated gently down to the ground.

It landed right on the spot where his aunt and uncle's old house had once stood. Everything was exactly like the owner remembered it. The air smelled of green leaves and warm woodsmoke, just like it did when he was a boy.

'I never thought how nice it would be to
live in the country,' the owner said to himself.
Then he took out his key and opened the door.